CONDITIONALLY HUMAN

CONDITIONALLY HUMAN

by Walter M. Miller, Jr.

They were such cute synthetic creatures, it was impossible not to love them. Of course, that was precisely why they were dangerous!

There was no use hanging around after breakfast. His wife was in a hurt mood, and he could neither endure the hurt nor remove it. He put on his coat in the kitchen and stood for a moment with his hat in his hands. His wife was still at the table, absently fingering the handle of her cup and staring fixedly out the window at the kennels behind the house. He moved quietly up behind her and touched her silk-clad shoulder. The shoulder shivered away from him, and her dark hair swung shiningly as she shuddered. He drew his hand back and his bewildered face went slack and miserable.

"Honeymoon's over, huh?"

She said nothing, but shrugged faintly.

"You knew I worked for the F.B.A.," he said. "You knew I'd have charge of a district pound. You knew it before we got married."

"I didn't know you killed them," she said venomously.

"I won't have to kill many. Besides, they're only animals."

"*Intelligent* animals!"

"Intelligent as a human imbecile, maybe."

"A small child is an imbecile. Would you kill a small child?"

"You're taking intelligence as the only criterion of humanity," he protested hopelessly, knowing that a logical defense was useless against sentimentality. "Baby—"

"Don't call me baby! Call *them* baby!"

Norris backed a few steps toward the door. Against his better judgment, he spoke again. "Anne honey, look! Think of the *good* things about the job. Sure, everything has its ugly angles. But think—we get this house rent-free; I've got my own district with no bosses around; I make my own hours; you'll meet lots of people that stop in at the pound. It's a *fine* job, honey!"

She sipped her coffee and appeared to be listening, so he went on.

"And what can I do? You know how the Federation handles employment. They looked over my aptitude tests and sent me to Bio-Administration. If I don't want to follow my aptitudes, the only choice is common labor. That's the *law*."

4

"I suppose you have an aptitude for killing babies?" she said sweetly.

Norris withered. His voice went desperate. "They assigned me to it because I *liked* babies. And because I have a B.S. in biology and an aptitude for dealing with people. Can't you understand? Destroying unclaimed units is the smallest part of it. Honey, before the evolvotron, before Anthropos went into the mutant-animal business, people used to elect dogcatchers. Think of it that way—I'm just a dogcatcher."

Her cool green eyes turned slowly to meet his gaze. Her face was delicately cut from cold marble. She was a small woman, slender and fragile, but her quiet contempt made her loom.

He backed closer to the door.

"Well, I've got to get on the job." He put on his hat and picked at a splinter on the door. He frowned studiously at the splinter. "I—I'll see you tonight." He ripped the splinter loose when it became obvious that she didn't want to be kissed.

He grunted a nervous good-by and stumbled down the hall and out of the house. The honeymoon was over, all right.

He climbed in the kennel-truck and drove east toward the highway. The suburban street wound among the pastel plasticoid cottages that were set approximately two to an acre on the lightly wooded land. With its population legally fixed at three hundred million, most of the country had become one big suburb, dotted with community centers and lined with narrow belts of industrial development. Norris wished there were someplace where he could be completely alone.

As he approached an intersection, he saw a small animal sitting on the curb, wrapped in its own bushy tail. Its oversized head was bald on top, but the rest of its body was covered with blue-gray fur. Its tiny pink tongue was licking daintily at small forepaws with prehensile thumbs. It was a cat-Q-5. It glanced curiously at the truck as Norris pulled to a halt.

He smiled at it from the window and called, "What's your name, kitten?"

The cat-Q-5 stared at him impassively for a moment, let out a stuttering high-pitched wail, then: "Kiyi Rorry."

"Whose child are you, Rorry?" he asked. "Where do you live?"

The cat-Q-5 took its time about answering. There were no houses near the intersection, and Norris feared that the animal might be lost. It blinked at him, sleepily bored, and resumed its paw-washing. He repeated the questions.

"Mama kiyi," said the cat-Q-5 disgustedly.

"That's right, Mama's kitty. But where is Mama? Do you suppose she ran away?"

The cat-Q-5 looked startled. It stuttered for a moment, and its fur crept slowly erect. It glanced around hurriedly, then shot off down the street at a fast scamper. He followed it in the truck until it darted onto a porch and began wailing through the screen, "Mama no run ray! Mama no run ray!"

Norris grinned and drove on. A class-C couple, allowed no children of their own, could get quite attached to a cat-Q-5. The felines were emotionally safer than the quasi-human chimp-K series called "neutroids." When a pet neutroid died, a family was broken with grief; but most couples could endure the death of a cat-Q or a dog-F. Class-C couples were allowed two lesser units or one neutroid.

His grin faded as he wondered which Anne would choose. The Norrises were class-C—defective heredity.

*

He found himself in Sherman III Community Center—eight blocks of commercial buildings, serving the surrounding suburbs. He stopped at the message office to pick up his mail. There was a memo from Chief Franklin. He tore it open nervously and read it in the truck. It was something he had been expecting for several days.

Attention All District Inspectors: Subject: Deviant Neutroid.

You will immediately begin a systematic and thorough survey of all animals whose serial numbers fall in the Bermuda-K-99 series for birth dates during July 2234. This is in connection with the Delmont Negligency Case. Seize all animals in this category, impound, and run proper sections of normalcy tests. Watch for mental and glandular deviation. Delmont has confessed to passing only one non-standard unit, but there may be others. He disclaims memory of deviant's serial number. This could be a ruse to bring a stop to investigations when one animal is found. Be thorough.

If allowed to reach age-set or adulthood, such a deviant could be dangerous to its owner or to others. Hold all seized K-99s who show the slightest abnormality in the normalcy tests. Forward to central lab. Return standard units to their owners. Accomplish entire survey project within seven days.

C. Franklin

Norris frowned at the last sentence. His district covered about two hundred square miles. Its replacement-quota of new neutroids was around three hundred animals a month. He tried to estimate how many of July's influx had been K-99s from Bermuda Factory. Forty, at least. Could he do it in a week? And there were only eleven empty neutroid cages in his kennel. The other forty-nine were occupied by the previous inspector's "unclaimed" inventory—awaiting destruction.

He wadded the memo in his pocket, then nosed the truck onto the highway and headed toward Wylo City and the district wholesale offices of Anthropos, Inc. They should be able to give him a list of all July's Bermuda K-99 serial numbers that had entered his territory, together with the retailers to whom the animals had been sold. A week's deadline for finding and testing forty neutroids would put him in a tight squeeze.

He was halfway to Wylo City when the radiophone buzzed on his dashboard. He pulled into the slow lane and answered quickly, hoping for Anne's voice. A polite professional purr came instead.

"Inspector Norris? This is Doctor Georges. We haven't met, but I imagine we will. Are you extremely busy at the moment?"

Norris hesitated. "Extremely," he said.

"Well, this won't take long. One of my patients—a Mrs. Sarah Glubbes—called a while ago and said her baby was sick. I must be getting absent-minded, because I forgot she was class C until I got there." He hesitated. "The baby turned out to be a neutroid. It's dying. Eighteenth order virus."

"So?"

"Well, she's—uh—rather a *peculiar* woman, Inspector. Keeps telling me how much trouble she had in childbirth, and how she can't ever have another one. It's pathetic. She *believes* it's her own. Do you understand?"

"I think so," Norris replied slowly. "But what do you want me to do? Can't you send the neutroid to a vet?"

"She insists it's going to a hospital. Worst part is that she's heard of the disease. Knows it can be cured with the proper treatment—in humans. Of course, no hospital would play along with her fantasy and take a neutroid, especially since she couldn't pay for its treatment."

"I still don't see—"

"I thought perhaps you could help me fake a substitution. It's a K-48 series, five-year-old, three-year set. Do you have one in the pound that's not claimed?"

Norris thought for a moment. "I think I have *one*. You're welcome to it, Doctor, but you can't fake a serial number. She'll know it. And even though they look exactly alike, the new one won't recognize her. It'll be spooky."

There was a long pause, followed by a sigh. "I'll try it anyway. Can I come get the animal now?"

"I'm on the highway—"

"Please, Norris! This is urgent. That woman will lose her mind completely if—"

"All right, I'll call my wife and tell her to open the pound for you. Pick out the K-48 and sign for it. And listen—"

"Yes?"

"Don't let me catch you falsifying a serial number."

Doctor Georges laughed faintly. "I won't, Norris. Thanks a million." He hung up quickly.

Norris immediately regretted his consent. It bordered on being illegal. But he saw it as a quick way to get rid of an animal that might later have to be killed.

He called Anne. Her voice was dull. She seemed depressed, but not angry. When he finished talking, she said, "All right, Terry," and hung up.

*

By noon, he had finished checking the shipping lists at the wholesale house in Wylo City. Only thirty-five of July's Bermuda-K-

99s had entered his territory, and they were about equally divided among five pet shops, three of which were in Wylo City.

After lunch, he called each of the retail dealers, read them the serial numbers, and asked them to check the sales records for names and addresses of individual buyers. By three o'clock, he had the entire list filled out, and the task began to look easier. All that remained was to pick up the thirty-five animals.

And *that*, he thought, was like trying to take a year-old baby away from its doting mother. He sighed and drove to the Wylo suburbs to begin his rounds.

Anne met him at the door when he came home at six. He stood on the porch for a moment, smiling at her weakly. The smile was not returned.

"Doctor Georges came," she told him. "He signed for the—" She stopped to stare at him. "Darling, your face! What happened?"

Gingerly he touch the livid welts down the side of his cheek. "Just scratched a little," he muttered. He pushed past her and went to the phone in the hall. He sat eying it distastefully for a moment, not liking what he had to do. Anne came to stand beside him and examine the scratches.

Finally he lifted the phone and dialed the Wylo exchange. A grating mechanical voice answered, "Locator center. Your party, please."

"Sheriff Yates," Norris grunted.

The robot operator, which had on tape the working habits of each Wylo City citizen, began calling numbers. It found the off-duty sheriff on its third try, in a Wylo pool hall.

"I'm getting so I hate that infernal gadget," Yates grumbled. "I think it's got me psyched. What do you want, Norris?"

"Cooperation. I'm mailing you three letters charging three Wylo citizens with resisting a Federal official—namely *me*—and charging one of them with assault. I tried to pick up their neutroids for a pound inspection—"

Yates bellowed lusty laughter into the phone.

"It's not funny. I've got to get those neutroids. It's in connection with the Delmont case."

Yates stopped laughing. "Oh. Well, I'll take care of it."

"It's a rush-order, Sheriff. Can you get the warrants tonight and pick up the animals in the morning?"

"Easy on those warrants, boy. Judge Charleman can't be disturbed just any time. I can get the newts to you by noon, I guess, provided we don't have to get a helicopter posse to chase down the mothers."

"That'll be all right. And listen, Yates—fix it so the charges will be dropped if they cooperate. Don't shake those warrants around unless they just won't listen to reason. But get those neutroids."

"Okay, boy. Gotcha."

Norris gave him the names and addresses of the three unwilling mothers. As soon as he hung up, Anne touched his shoulders and said, "Sit still." She began smoothing a chilly ointment over his burning cheek.

"Hard day?" she asked.

"Not too hard. Those were just three out of fifteen. I got the other twelve. They're in the truck."

"That's good," she said. "You've got only twelve empty cages."

He neglected to tell her that he had stopped at twelve for just this reason. "Guess I better get them unloaded," he said, standing up.

"Can I help you?"

He stared at her for a moment, saying nothing. She smiled a little and looked aside. "Terry, I'm sorry—about this morning. I—I know you've got a job that has to be—" Her lip quivered slightly.

Norris grinned, caught her shoulders, and pulled her close.

"Honeymoon's on again, huh?" she whispered against his neck.

"Come on," he grunted. "Let's unload some neutroids, before I forget all about work."

*

They went out to the kennels together. The cages were inside a sprawling concrete barn, which was divided into three large rooms—one for the fragile neuter humanoid creatures, and another for the lesser mutants, such as cat-Qs, dog-Fs, dwarf bears, and foot-high lambs that never matured into sheep. The third room contained a small gas chamber with a conveyor belt leading from it to a crematory-incinerator.

10

Norris kept the third locked lest his wife see its furnishings.

The doll-like neutroids began their mindless chatter as soon as their keepers entered the building. Dozens of blazing blond heads began dancing about their cages. Their bodies thwacked against the wire mesh as they leaped about their compartments with monkey grace.

Their human appearance was broken by only two distinct features: short beaverlike tails decorated with fluffy curls of fur, and an erect thatch of scalp-hair that grew up into a bright candleflame. Otherwise, they appeared completely human, with baby-pink skin, quick little smiles, and cherubic faces. They were sexually neuter and never grew beyond a predetermined age-set which varied for each series. Age-sets were available from one to ten years human equivalent. Once a neutroid reached its age-set, it remained at the set's child-development level until death.

"They must be getting to know you pretty well," Anne said, glancing around at the cages.

Norris was wearing a slight frown as he inspected the room. "They've never gotten this excited before."

He walked along a row of cages, then stopped by a K-76 to stare.

"*Apple cores!*" He turned to face his wife. "How did apples get in there?"

She reddened. "I felt sorry for them, eating that goo from the mechanical feeder. I drove down to Sherman III and bought six dozen cooking apples."

"That was a mistake."

She frowned irritably. "We can afford it."

"That's not the point. There's a reason for the mechanical feeders." He paused, wondering how he could tell her the truth. He blundered on: "They get to love whoever feeds them."

"I can't see—"

"How would you feel about disposing of something that loved you?"

Anne folded her arms and stared at him. "Planning to dispose of any soon?" she asked acidly.

"Honeymoon's off again, eh?"

She turned away. "I'm sorry, Terry. I'll try not to mention it again."

He began unloading the truck, pulling the frightened and squirming doll-things forth one at a time with a snare-pole. They were one-man pets, always frightened of strangers.

"What's the Delmont case, Terry?" Anne asked while he worked.

"Huh?"

"I heard you mention it on the phone. Anything to do with why you got your face scratched?"

He nodded sourly. "Indirectly, yes. It's a long story."

"Tell me."

"Well, Delmont was a green-horn evolvotron operator at the Bermuda plant. His job was taking the unfertilized chimpanzee ova out of the egg-multiplier, mounting them in his machine, and bombarding the gene structure with sub-atomic particles. It's tricky business. He flashes a huge enlargement of the ovum on the electron microscope screen—large enough so he can see the individual protein molecules. He has an artificial gene pattern to compare it with. It's like shooting sub-atomic billiards. He's got to fire alpha-particles into the gene structure and displace certain links by just the right amount. And he's got to be quick about it before the ovum dies from an overdose of radiation from the enlarger. A good operator can get one success out of seven tries.

"Well, Delmont worked a week and spoiled over a hundred ova without a single success. They threatened to fire him. I guess he got hysterical. Anyway, he reported one success the next day. It was faked. The ovum had a couple of flaws—something wrong in the central nervous system's determinants, and in the glandular makeup. Not a standard neutroid ovum. He passed it on to the incubators to get a credit, knowing it wouldn't be caught until after birth."

"It wasn't caught at all?" Anne asked.

"Funny thing, he was afraid it wouldn't be. He got to worrying about it, thought maybe a mental-deviant would pass, and that it might be dangerous. So he went back to its incubator and cut off the hormone flow into its compartment."

"Why that?"

"So it *would* develop sexuality. A neutroid would be born a female if they didn't give it suppressive doses of male hormone prenatally.

That keeps ovaries from developing and it comes out neuter. But Delmont figured a female would be caught and stopped before the final inspection. They'd dispose of her without even bothering to examine for the other defects. And he could blame the sexuality on an equipment malfunction. He thought it was pretty smart. Trouble was they didn't catch the female. She went on through; they all *look* female."

"How did they find out about it now?"

"He got caught last month, trying it again. And he confessed to doing it once before. No telling how many times he *really* did it."

Norris held up the final kicking, squealing, tassel-haired doll from the back of the kennel-truck. He grinned at his wife. "This little fellow, for instance. It might be a potential she. It might also be a potential murderer. *All* these kiddos are from the machines in the section where Delmont worked."

Anne snorted and caught the baby-creature in her arms. It struggled and tried to bite, but subsided a little when she disentangled it from the snare. "Kkr-r-reee," it cooed nervously. "Kkr-r-reee!"

"You tell him you're no murderer," Anne purred to it.

Norris watched disapprovingly while she fondled it. One thing he had learned: to steer clear of emotional attachments. It was eight months old and looked like a child of two years—a year short of its age-set. And it was designed to be as affectionate as a human child.

"Put it in the cage, Anne," he said quietly.

She looked up and shook her head.

"It belongs to somebody else. If it fixes a libido attachment on you, you're actually robbing its owner. They can't love many people at once."

She snorted, but installed the thing in its cage.

"Anne—" Norris hesitated, hating to approach the subject. "Do you—want one—for yourself? I can sign an unclaimed one over to you to keep in the house. It won't cost us anything."

Slowly she shook her head, and her pale eyes went moody and luminous. "I'm going to have one of my own," she said.

He stood in the back of the truck, staring down at her. "Do you realize what—"

"I know what I'm saying. We're class-C on account of heart-trouble in both our families. Well, I don't care, Terry. I'm not going to waste a heart over one of these pathetic little artificial animals. We're going to have a baby."

"You know what they'd do to us?"

"If they catch us, yes—compulsory divorce, sterilization. But they won't catch us. I'll have it at home, Terry. Not even a doctor. We'll hide it."

"I won't let you do such a thing."

She faced him angrily. "Oh, this whole rotten *world!*" she choked. Suddenly she turned and fled out of the building. She was sobbing.

*

Norris climbed slowly down from the truck and wandered on into the house. She was not in the kitchen nor the living room. The bedroom door was locked. He shrugged and went to sit on the sofa. The television set was on, and a newscast was coming from a local station.

"... we were unable to get shots of the body," the announcer was saying. "But here is a view of the Georges residence. I'll switch you to our mobile unit in Sherman II, James Duncan reporting."

Norris frowned with bewilderment as the scene shifted to a two-story plasticoid house among the elm trees. It was after dark, but the mobile unit's powerful floodlights made daylight of the house and its yard and the police 'copters sitting in a side lot. An ambulance was parked in the street. A new voice came on the audio.

"This is James Duncan, ladies and gentlemen, speaking to you from our mobile unit in front of the late Doctor Hiram Georges' residence just west of Sherman II. We are waiting for the stretcher to be brought out, and Police Chief Erskine Miler is standing here beside me to give us a word about the case. Doctor Georges' death has shocked the community deeply. Most of you local listeners have known him for many years—some of you have depended upon his services as a family physician. He was a man well known, well loved. But now let's listen to Chief Miler."

Norris sat breathing quickly. There could scarcely be two Doctor Georges in the community, but only this morning....

A growling drawl came from the audio. "This's Chief Miler speaking, folks. I just want to say that if any of you know the whereabouts of a Mrs. Sarah Glubbes, call me immediately. She's wanted for questioning."

"Thank you, Chief. This is James Duncan again. I'll review the facts for you briefly again, ladies and gentlemen. At seven o'clock, less than an hour ago, a woman—allegedly Mrs. Glubbes—burst into Doctor Georges' dining room while the family was at dinner. She was brandishing a pistol and screaming, 'You stole my baby! You gave me the wrong baby! Where's my baby?'

"When the doctor assured her that there was no other baby, she fired, shattering his salad plate. Glancing off it, the bullet pierced his heart. The woman fled. A peculiar feature of the case is that Mrs. Glubbes, the alleged intruder, *has no baby*. Just a minute—just a minute—here comes the stretcher now."

Norris turned the set off and went to call the police. He told them what he knew and promised to make himself available for questioning if it became necessary. When he turned from the phone, Anne was standing in the bedroom doorway. She might have been crying a little, but she concealed it well.

"What was all that?" she asked.

"Woman killed a man. I happened to know the motive."

"What was it?"

"Neutroid trouble."

"You meet up with a lot of unpleasantness in this business, don't you?"

"Lot of unpleasant emotions tangled up in it," he admitted.

"I know. Well, supper's been keeping hot for two hours. Shall we eat?"

*

They went to bed at midnight, but it was after one when he became certain that his wife was asleep. He lay in darkness for a time, listening to her even breathing. Then he cautiously eased himself out of bed and tiptoed quietly through the door, carrying his shoes and trousers. He put them on in the kitchen and stole silently out to the kennels. A half moon hung low in a misty sky, and the wind was chilly out of the north.

He went into the neutroid room and flicked a switch. A few sleepy chatters greeted the light.

One at a time, he awoke twenty-three of the older doll-things and carried them to a large glass-walled compartment. These were the long-time residents; they knew him well, and they came with him willingly—like children after the Piper of Hamlin. When he had gotten them in the glass chamber, he sealed the door and turned on the gas. The conveyor would automatically carry them on to the incinerator.

Now he had enough cages for the Bermuda-K-99s.

He hurriedly quit the kennels and went to sit on the back steps. His eyes were burning, but the thought of tears made him sicker. It was like an assassin crying while he stabbed his victim. It was more honest just to retch.

When he tiptoed back inside, he got as far as the hall. Then he saw Anne's small figure framed in the bedroom window, silhouetted against the moonlit yard. She had slipped into her negligee and was sitting on the narrow windowstool, staring silently out at the dull red tongue of exhaust gases from the crematory's chimney.

Norris backed away. He went to the parlor and lay down on the couch.

After a while he heard her come into the room. She paused in the center of the rug, a fragile mist in the darkness. He turned his face away and waited for the rasping accusation. But soon she came to sit on the edge of the sofa. She said nothing. Her hand crept out and touched his cheek lightly. He felt her cool finger-tips trace a soft line up his temple.

"It's all right, Terry," she whispered.

He kept his face averted. Her fingers traced a last stroke. Then she padded quietly back to the bedroom. He lay awake until dawn, knowing that it would never be all right, neither the creating nor the killing, until he—and the whole world—completely lost sanity. And then everything would be all right, only it still wouldn't make sense.

*

16

CONDITIONALLY HUMAN

Anne was asleep when he left the house. The night mist had gathered into clouds that made a gloomy morning of it. He drove on out in the kennel-truck, meaning to get the rest of the Bermuda-K-99s so that he could begin his testing.

Still he felt the night's guilt, like a sticky dew that refused to depart with morning. Why should he have to kill the things? The answer was obvious. Society manufactured them because killing them was permissible. Human babies could not be disposed of when the market became glutted. The neutroids offered solace to childless women, kept them satisfied with a restricted birth rate. And why a restricted birth rate? Because by keeping the population at five billions, the Federation could insure a decent living standard for everybody.

Where there was giving, Norris thought glumly, there was also taking away. Man had always deluded himself by thinking that he "created," but he created nothing. He thought that he had created—with his medical science and his end to wars—a longer life for the individual. But he found that he had only taken the lives of the unborn and added them to the years of the aged. Man now had a life expectancy of eighty, except that he had damn little chance of being born to enjoy it.

A neutroid filled the cradle in his stead. A neutroid that never ate as much, or grew up to be unemployed. A neutroid could be killed if things got tough, but could still satisfy a woman's craving to mother something small.

Norris gave up thinking about it. Eventually he would have to adjust to it. He was already adjusted to a world that loved the artificial mutants as children. He had been brought up in it. Emotion came in conflict with the grim necessities of his job. Somehow he would have to love them in the parlor and kill them in the kennel. It was only a matter of adjustment.

*

At noon, he brought back another dozen K-99s and installed them in his cages. There had been two highly reluctant mothers, but he skipped them and left the seizure to the local authorities. Yates had already brought in the three from yesterday.

"No more scratches?" Anne asked him while they ate lunch. They did not speak of the night's mass-disposal.

Norris smiled mechanically. "I learned my lesson yesterday. If they bare their fangs, I get out without another word. Funny thing though—I've got a feeling one mother pulled a fast one."

"What happened?"

"Well, I told her what I wanted and why. She didn't like it, but she let me in. I started out with her newt, but she wanted a receipt. So I gave her one; took the serial number off my checklist. She looked at it and said, 'Why, that's not Chichi's number!' I looked at the newt's foot, and sure enough it wasn't. I had to leave it. It was a K-99, but not even from Bermuda."

"I thought they were all registered," Anne said.

"They are. I told her she had the wrong neutroid, but she got mad. Went and got the sales receipt. It checked with her newt, and it was from O'Reilley's pet shop—right place, wrong number. I just don't get it."

"Nothing to worry about, is it Terry?"

He looked at her peculiarly. "Ever think what might happen if someone started a black market in neutroids?"

They finished the meal in silence. After lunch he went out again to gather up the rest of the group. By four o'clock, he had gotten all that were to be had without the threat of a warrant. The screams and pleas and tears of the owners left him gloomily despising himself.

If Delmont's falsification had been widespread, he might have to turn several of the thirty-five over to central lab for dissection and ultimate destruction. That would bring the murderous wrath of their owners down upon him. He began to understand why bio-inspectors were frequently shifted from one territory to another.

On the way home, he stopped in Sherman II to check on the missing number. It was the largest of the Sherman communities, covering fifty blocks of commercial buildings. He parked in the outskirts and took a sidewalk escalator toward O'Reilley's address.

It was on a dingy sidestreet, reminiscent of past centuries, a street of small bars and bowling alleys and cigar stores. There was even a shop with three gold balls above the entrance, but the place was now an antique store. A light mist was falling when he stepped off the escalator and stood in front of the pet shop. A sign hung out over the sidewalk, announcing:

J. "DOGGY" O'REILLEY
PETS FOR SALE
DUMB BLONDES AND GOLDFISH
MUTANTS FOR THE CHILDLESS
BUY A BUNDLE OF JOY

Norris frowned at the sign and wandered inside. The place was warm and gloomy. He wrinkled his nose at the strong musk of animal odors. O'Reilley's was not a shining example of cleanliness.

Somewhere a puppy was yapping, and a parrot croaked the lyrics of *A Chimp to Call My Own*, which Norris recognized as the theme song of a popular soap-opera about a lady evolvotron operator.

He paused briefly by a tank of silk-draped goldfish. The shop had a customer. An elderly lady was haggling with a wizened manager over the price of a half grown second-hand dog-F. She was shaking her last dog's death certificate under his nose and demanding a guarantee of the dog's alleged F-5 intelligence. The old man offered to swear on a Bible, but he demurred when it came to swearing on a ledger.

The dog was saying, "Don' sell me, Dada. Don' sell me."

Norris smiled sardonically to himself. The non-human pets were smarter than the neutroids. A K-108 could speak a dozen words, and a K-99 never got farther than "mamma," "pappa," and "cookie." Anthropos was afraid to make the quasi-humans too intelligent, lest sentimentalists proclaim them really human.

He wandered on toward the back of the building, pausing briefly by the cash register to inspect O'Reilley's license, which hung in a dusty frame on the wall behind the counter. "James Fallon O'Reilley ... authorized dealer in mutant animals ... all non-predatory mammals including chimpanzee-K series ... license expires June 1, 2235."

It seemed in order, although the expiration date was approaching. He started toward a bank of neutroid cages along the opposite wall, but O'Reilley was mincing across the floor to meet him. The customer had gone. The little manager wore an elfin professional smile, and his bald head bobbled in a welcoming nod.

19

"Good day, sir, good day! May I show you a dwarf kangaroo, or a—" He stopped and adjusted his spectacles. He blinked and peered as Norris flashed his badge. His smile waned.

"I'm Agent Norris, Mr. O'Reilley. Called you yesterday for that rundown on K-99 sales."

O'Reilley looked suddenly nervous. "Oh, yes. Find 'em all?"

Norris shook his head. "No. That's why I stopped by. There's some mistake on—" he glanced at his list—"on K-99-LJZ-351. Let's check it again."

O'Reilley seemed to cringe. "No mistake. I gave you the buyer's name."

"She has a different number."

"Can I help it if she traded with somebody?"

"She didn't. She bought it here. I saw the receipt."

"Then she traded with one of my other customers!" snapped the old man.

"Two of your customers have the same name—Adelia Schultz? Not likely. Let's see your duplicate receipt book."

O'Reilley's wrinkled face set itself into a stubborn mask. "Doubt if it's still around."

Norris frowned. "Look, pop, I've had a rough day. I *could* start naming some things around here that need fixing—sanitary violations and such. Not to mention that sign—'dumb blondes.' They outlawed that one when they executed that shyster doctor for shooting K-108s full of growth hormones, trying to raise himself a harem to sell. Besides, you're required to keep sales records until they've been micro-filmed. There hasn't been a microfilming since July."

The wrinkled face twitched with frustrated anger. O'Reilley shuffled to the counter while Norris followed. He got a fat binder from under the register and started toward a wooden stairway.

"Where you going?" Norris called.

"Get my old glasses," the manager grumbled. "Can't see through these new things."

"Leave the book here and *I'll* check it," Norris offered.

But O'Reilley was already limping quickly up the stairs. He seemed not to hear. He shut the door behind him, and Norris heard the lock click. The bio-agent waited. Again the thought of a black market troubled him. Unauthorized neutroids could mean lots of trouble.

*

Five minutes passed before the old man came down the stairs. He said nothing as he placed the book on the counter. Norris noticed that his hands were trembling as he shuffled through the pages.

"Let *me* look," said the bio-agent.

O'Reilley stepped reluctantly aside. Norris had memorized the owner's receipt number, and he found the duplicate quickly. He stared at it silently. "Mrs. Adele Schultz ... chimpanzee-K-99-LJZ-351." It was the number of the animal he wanted, but it wasn't the number on Mrs. Schultz's neutroid nor on her original copy of the receipt.

He held the book up to his eye and aimed across the page at the light. O'Reilley's breathing became audible. Norris put the book down, folded two thicknesses of handkerchief over the blade of his pocketknife, and ran it down the seam between the pages. He took the sheet he wanted, folded it, and stowed it in his vest pocket. O'Reilley was stuttering angrily.

Norris turned to face him coldly. "Nice erasure job, for a carbon copy."

The old man prepared himself for exploding. Norris quietly put on his hat.

"See you in court, O'Reilley."

"*Wait!*"

Norris turned. "Okay, I'm waiting."

The old man sagged into a deflated bag of wrinkles. "Let's sit down first," he said weakly.

Norris followed him up the stairs and into a dingy parlor. The tiny apartment smelled of boiled cabbage and sweat. An orange-haired neutroid lay asleep on a small rug in a corner. Norris knelt beside it and read the tattooed figures on the sole of its left foot—K-99-LJZ-351. Somehow he was not surprised.

When he stood up, the old man was sagged in an ancient armchair, his head propped on a hand that covered his eyes.

"Lots of good explanations, I guess?" Norris asked quietly.

21

"Not good ones."

"Let's hear them, anyway."

O'Reilley sighed and straightened. He blinked at the inspector and spoke in a monotone. "My missus died five years back. We were class-B—allowed one child of our own—if we could have one. We couldn't. But since we were class-B, we couldn't own a neutroid either. Sorta got around it by running a pet shop. Mary—she always cried when we sold a neut. I sorta felt bad about it myself. But we never did swipe one. Last year this Bermuda shipment come in. I sold most of 'em pretty quick, but Peony here—she was kinda puny. Seemed like nobody wanted her. Kept her around so long, I got attached to her. 'Fraid somebody'd buy her. So I faked the receipt and moved her up here."

"That all?"

The old man nodded.

"Ever done this before?"

He shook his head.

Norris let a long silence pass while he struggled with himself. At last he said, "Your license could be revoked, you know."

"I know."

Norris ground his fist thoughtfully in his palm and stared at the sleeping doll-thing. "I'll take your books home with me tonight," he said. "I want to make a complete check for similar changes. Any objections?"

"None. It's the only trick I've pulled, so help me."

"If that's true, I won't report you. We'll just attach a correction to that page, and you'll put the newt back in stock." He hesitated. "Providing it's not a deviant. I'll have to take it in for examination."

A choking sound came from the armchair. Norris stared curiously at the old man. Moisture was creeping in the wrinkles around his eyes.

"Something the matter?"

O'Reilley nodded. "She's a deviant."

"How do you know?"

The dealer pulled himself erect and hobbled to the sleeping neutroid. He knelt beside it and stroked a small bare shoulder gently.

"Peony," he breathed. "Peony, girl—wake up."

Its fluffy tail twitched for a moment. Then it sat up, rubbing its eyes and yawning. It *looked* normal, like a two-year-old girl with soft brown eyes. It pouted at O'Reilley for awakening it. It saw Norris and ignored him, apparently too sleepy to be frightened.

"How's my Peony-girl?" the dealer purred.

It licked its lips. "Wanna g'ass o' water, Daddy," it said drowsily.

Norris caught his breath. No K-99 should be able to make a speech that long, even when it reached the developmental limit. He glanced at O'Reilley. The old man nodded slowly, then went to the kitchen for a glass of water. She drank greedily and eyed her foster-parent.

"Daddy crying."

O'Reilley glowered at her and blew his nose solemnly. "Don't be silly, child. Now get your coat on and go with Mister Norris. He's taking you for a ride in his truck. Won't that be fine?"

"I don't want to. I wanna stay here."

"*Peeony!* On with you!"

She brought her coat and stared at Norris with childish contempt. "Can Daddy go, too?"

"Be on your way!" growled O'Reilley. "I got things to do."

"We're coming back?"

"Of course you're coming back! *Git* now—or shall I get my spanking switch?"

Peony strolled out the door ahead of Norris.

"Oh, inspector, would you be punching the night latch for me as you leave the shop? I think I'll be closing for the day."

Norris paused at the head of the stairs, looking back at the old man. But O'Reilley closed himself inside and the lock clicked. The agent sighed and glanced down at the small being beside him.

"Want me to carry you, Peony?"

She sniffed disdainfully. She hopped upon the banister and slid down ahead of him. Her motor-responses were typically neutroid—something like a monkey, something like a squirrel. But there was no question about it; she was one of Delmont's deviants. He wondered what they would do with her in central lab. He could remember no instance of an intelligent mutant getting into the market.

Somehow he could not consign her to a cage in the back of the truck. He drove home while she sat beside him on the front seat. She watched the scenery and remained aloof, occasionally looking around to ask, "Can we go back now?"

Norris could not bring himself to answer.

*

When he got home, he led her into the house and stopped in the hall to call Chief Franklin. The operator said, "His office doesn't answer, sir. Shall I give you the robot locator?"

Norris hesitated. His wife came into the hall. She stooped to grin at Peony, and Peony said, "Do you live here, too?" Anne gasped and sat on the floor to stare.

Norris said, "Cancel the call. It'll wait till tomorrow." He dropped the phone quickly.

"What series is it?" Anne asked excitedly. "I never saw one that could talk."

"*It* is a *she*," he said. "And she's a series unto herself. Some of Delmont's work."

Peony was looking from one to the other of them with a baffled face. "Can we go back now?"

Norris shook his head. "You're going to spend the night with us, Peony," he said softly. "Your daddy wants you to."

His wife was watching him thoughtfully. Norris looked aside and plucked nervously at a corner of the telephone book. Suddenly she caught Peony's hand and led her toward the kitchen.

"Come on, baby, let's go find a cookie or something."

Norris started out the front door, but in a moment Anne was back. She caught at his collar and tugged. "Not so fast!"

He turned to frown. Her face accused him at a six-inch range.

"Just what do you think you're going to do with that child?"

He was silent for a long time. "You know what I'm *supposed* to do."

Her unchanging stare told him that she wouldn't accept any evasions. "I heard you trying to get your boss on the phone."

"I canceled it, didn't I?"

"Until tomorrow."

He worked his hands nervously. "I don't know, honey—I just don't know."

"They'd kill her at central lab, wouldn't they?"

"Well, they'd need her as evidence in Delmont's trial."

"They'd kill her, wouldn't they?"

"When it was over—it's hard to say. The law says deviants must be destroyed, but—"

"Well?"

He paused miserably. "We've got a few days to think about it, honey. I don't have to make my report for a week."

He sidled out the door. Looking back, he saw the hard determination in her eyes as she watched him. He knew somehow that he was going to lose either his job or his wife. Maybe both. He shuffled moodily out to the kennels to care for his charges.

*

A great silence filled the house during the evening. Supper was a gloomy meal. Only Peony spoke; she sat propped on two cushions at the table, using her silver with remarkable skill.

Norris wondered about her intelligence. Her chronological age was ten months; her physical age was about two years; but her mental age seemed to compare favorably with at least a three year old.

Once he reached across the table to touch her forehead. She eyed him curiously for a moment and continued eating. Her temperature was warmer than human, but not too warm for the normally high neutroid metabolism—somewhere around 101°. The rapid rate of maturation made I.Q. determination impossible.

"You've got a good appetite, Peony," Anne remarked.

"I like Daddy's cooking better," she said with innocent bluntness. "When can I go home?"

Anne looked at Norris and waited for an answer. He managed a smile at the flame-haired cherub. "Tell you what we'll do. I'll call your daddy on the phone and let you say hello. Would you like that?"

She giggled, then nodded. "Uh-huh! When can we do it?"

"Later."

Anne tapped her fork thoughtfully against the edge of her plate. "I think we better have a nice long talk tonight, Terry," she said.

"Is there anything to talk about?" He pushed the plate away. "I'm not hungry."

*

He left the table and went to sit in darkness by the parlor window, while his wife did the dishes and Peony played with a handful of walnuts on the kitchen floor.

He watched the scattered lights of the suburbs and tried to think of nothing. The lights were peaceful, glimmering through the trees.

Once there had been no lights, only the flickering campfires of hunters shivering in the forest, when the world was young and sparsely planted with the seed of Man. Now the world was infected with his lights, and with the sound of his engines and the roar of his rockets. He had inherited the Earth and had filled it—too full.

There was no escape. His rockets had touched two of the planets, but even the new worlds offered no sanctuary for the unborn. Man could have babies—if allowed—faster than he could build ships to haul them away. He could only choose between a higher death rate and a lower birth rate.

And unborn children were not eligible to vote when Man made his choice.

His choice had robbed his wife of a biological need, and so he made a disposable baby with which to pacify her. He gave it a tail and only half a mind, so that it could not be confused with his own occasional children.

But Peony had only the tail. Still she was not born of the seed of Man. Strange seed, out of the jungle, warped toward the human pole, but still not human.

*

Norris heard a car approaching in the street. Its headlights swung along the curb, and it slowed to a halt in front of the house. A tall, slender man in a dark suit climbed out and stood for a moment, staring toward the house. He was only a shadow in the faint street light. Norris could not place him. Suddenly the man snapped on a flashlight and played it over the porch. Norris caught his breath and

26

darted toward the kitchen. Anne stared at him questioningly, while Peony peered up from her play.

He stooped beside her. "Listen, child!" he said quickly. "Do you know what a neutroid is?"

She nodded slowly. "They play in cages. They don't talk."

"Can you pretend you're a neutroid?"

"I can play neutroid. I play neutroid with Daddy sometimes, when people come to see him. He gives me candy when I play it. When can I go home?"

"Not now. There's a man coming to see us. Can you play neutroid for me? We'll give you lots of candy. Just don't talk. Pretend you're asleep."

"Now?"

"Now." He heard the door chimes ringing.

"Who is it?" Anne asked.

"I don't know. He may have the wrong house. Take Peony in the bedroom. I'll answer it."

His wife caught the child-thing up in her arms and hurried away. The chimes sounded again. Norris stalked down the hall and switched on the porch-light. The visitor was an elderly man, erect in his black suit and radiating dignity. As he smiled and nodded, Norris noticed his collar. A clergyman. Must have the wrong place, Norris thought.

"Are you Inspector Norris?"

The agent nodded, not daring to talk.

"I'm Father Paulson. I'm calling on behalf of a James O'Reilley. I think you know him. May I come in?"

Grudgingly, Norris swung open the door. "If you can stand the smell of paganism, come on in."

The priest chuckled politely. Norris led him to the parlor and turned on the light. He waved toward a chair.

"What's this all about? Does O'Reilley want something?"

Paulson smiled at the inspector's brusque tone and settled himself in the chair. "O'Reilley is a sick man," he said.

The inspector frowned. "He didn't look it to me."

"Sick of heart, Inspector. He came to me for advice. I couldn't give him any. He told me the story—about this Peony. I came to have a look at her, if I may."

Norris said nothing for a moment. O'Reilley had better keep his mouth shut, he thought, especially around clergymen. Most of them took a dim view of the whole mutant business.

"I didn't think you'd associate with O'Reilley," he said. "I thought you people excommunicated everybody that owns a neutroid. O'Reilley owns a whole shopful."

"That's true. But who knows? He might get rid of his shop. May I see this neutroid?"

"Why?"

"O'Reilley said it could talk. Is that true or is O'Reilley suffering delusions? That's what I came to find out."

"Neutroids don't talk."

The priest stared at him for a time, then nodded slowly, as if approving something. "You can rest assured," he said quietly, "that I'll say nothing of this visit, that I'll speak to no one about this creature."

Norris looked up to see his wife watching them from the doorway.

"Get Peony," he said.

"It's true then?" Paulson asked.

"I'll let you see for yourself."

Anne brought the small child-thing into the room and set her on the floor. Peony saw the visitor, chattered with fright, and bounded upon the back of the sofa to sit and scold. She was playing her game well, Norris thought.

The priest watched her with quiet interest. "Hello, little one."

Peony babbled gibberish. Paulson kept his eyes on her every movement. Suddenly he said, "I just saw your daddy, Peony. He wanted me to talk to you."

Her babbling ceased. The spell of the game was ended. Her eyes went sober. Then she looked at Norris and pouted. "I don't want any candy. I wanna go home."

Norris let out a deep breath. "I didn't say she couldn't talk," he pointed out sullenly.

"I didn't say you did," said Paulson. "You invited me to see for myself."

Anne confronted the clergyman. "What do you want?" she demanded. "The child's death? Did you come to assure yourself that she'd be turned over to the lab? I know your kind! You'd do anything to get rid of neutroids!"

"I came only to assure myself that O'Reilley's sane," Paulson told her.

"I don't believe you," she snapped.

He stared at her in wounded surprise; then he chuckled. "People used to trust the cloth. Ah, well. Listen, my child, you have us wrong. We say it's evil to create the creatures. We say *also* that it's evil to destroy them after they're made. Not murder, exactly, but—mockery of life, perhaps. It's the entire institution that's evil. Do you understand? As for this small creature of O'Reilley's—well, I hardly know what to make of her, but I certainly wouldn't wish her—uh—d-e-a-d."

Peony was listening solemnly to the conversation. Somehow Norris sensed a disinterested friend, if not an ally, in the priest. He looked at his wife. Her eyes were still suspicious.

"Tell me, Father," Norris asked, "if you were in my position, what would you do?"

Paulson fumbled with a button of his coat and stared at the floor while he pondered. "I wouldn't be in your position, young man. But if I were, I think I'd withhold her from my superiors. I'd also quit my job and go away."

It wasn't what Norris wanted to hear. But his wife's expression suddenly changed; she looked at the priest with a new interest. "And give Peony back to O'Reilley," she added.

"I shouldn't be giving you advice," he said unhappily. "I'm duty-bound to ask O'Reilley to give up his business and have nothing further to do with neutroids."

"But Peony's *human*," Anne argued. "She's *different*."

"I fail to agree."

"What!" Anne confronted him again. "What makes *you* human?"

"A soul, my child."

Anne put her hands on her hips and leaned forward to glare down at him like something unwholesome. "Can you put a voltmeter between your ears and measure it?"

The priest looked helplessly at Norris.

"*No!*" she said. "And you can't do it to Peony either!"

"Perhaps I had better go," Paulson said to his host.

Norris sighed. "Maybe you better, Padre. You found out what you wanted to know."

Anne stalked angrily out of the room, her dark hair swishing like a battle-pennant with each step. When the priest was gone, Norris picked up the child and held her in his lap. She was shivering with fright, as if she understood what had been said. Love them in the parlor, he thought, and kill them in the kennels.

"Can I go home? Doesn't Daddy want me any more?"

"Sure he does, baby. You just be good and everything'll be all right."

*

Norris felt a bad taste in his mouth as he laid her sleeping body on the sofa half an hour later. Everything was all wrong and it promised to remain that way. He couldn't give her back to O'Reilley, because she would be caught again when the auditor came to microfilm the records. And he certainly couldn't keep her himself—not with other Bio-agents wandering in and out every few days. She could not be concealed in a world where there were no longer any sparsely populated regions. There was nothing to do but obey the law and turn her over to Franklin's lab.

He closed his eyes and shuddered. If he did that, he could do anything—stomach anything—adapt to any vicious demands society made of him. If he sent the child away to die, he would know that he had attained an "objective" outlook. And what more could he want from life than adaptation and objectivity?

Well—his wife, for one thing.

He left the child on the sofa, turned out the light, and wandered into the bedroom. Anne was in bed, reading. She did not look up when she said, "Terry, if you let that baby be destroyed, I'll...."

"Don't say it," he cut in. "Any time you feel like leaving, you just leave. But don't threaten me with it."

She watched him silently for a moment. Then she handed him the newspaper she had been reading. It was folded around an advertisement.

*

BIOLOGISTS WANTED
by
ANTHROPOS INCORPORATED
for
Evolvotron Operators
Incubator Tenders
Nursery Supervisors
Laboratory Personnel
in
NEW ATLANTA PLANT
Call or write: Personnel Mgr.
ANTHROPOS INC.
Atlanta, Ga.
Note: Secure Work Department
release from present job
before applying.

*

He looked at Anne curiously. "So?"

She shrugged. "So there's a job, if you want to quit this one."

"What's this got to do with Peony, if anything?"

"We could take her with us."

"Not a chance," he said. "Do you suppose a talking neutroid would be any safer there?"

She demanded angrily, "Why should they want to destroy her?"

Norris sat on the edge of the bed and thought about it. "No particular *individual* wants to, honey. It's the law."

"But *why?*"

"Generally, because deviants are unknown quantities. They can be dangerous."

"That child—*dangerous?*"

"Dangerous to a concept, a vague belief that Man is something special, a closed tribe. And in a practical sense, she's dangerous because she's not a neuter. The Federation insists that all mutants be neuter and infertile, so it can control the mutant population. If mutants started reproducing, that could be a real threat in a world whose economy is so delicately balanced."

"Well, you're not going to let them have her, do you hear me?"

"I hear you," he grumbled.

*

On the following day, he went down to police headquarters to sign a statement concerning the motive in Doctor Georges' murder. As a result, Mrs. Glubbes was put away in the psycho-ward.

"It's funny, Norris," said Chief Miler, "what people'll do over a neutroid. Like Mrs. Glubbes thinking that newt was her own. I sure don't envy you your job. It's a wonder you don't get your head blown off. You must have an iron stomach."

Norris signed the paper and looked up briefly. "Sure, Chief. Just a matter of adaptation."

"Guess so." Miler patted his paunch and yawned. "How you coming on this Delmont business? Picked up any deviants yet?"

Norris laid down the pen abruptly. "No! Of course not! What made you think I had?"

Miler stopped in the middle of his yawn and stared at Norris curiously. "Touchy, aren't you?" he asked thoughtfully. "When I get that kind of answer from a prisoner, I right away start thinking—"

"Save it for your interrogation room," Norris growled. He stalked quickly out of the office while Chief Miler tapped his pencil absently and stared after him.

He was angry with himself for his indecision. He had to make a choice and make it soon. He was climbing in his car when a voice called after him from the building. He looked back to see Chief Miler trotting down the steps, his pudgy face glistening in the morning sun.

"Hey, Norris! Your missus is on the phone. Says it's urgent."

Norris went back grudgingly. A premonition of trouble gripped him.

"Phone's right there," the chief said, pointing with a stubby thumb.

The receiver lay on the desk, and he could hear it saying, "Hello—hello—" before he picked it up.

"Anne? What's the matter?"

Her voice was low and strained, trying to be cheerful. "Nothing's the matter, darling. We have a visitor. Come right home, will you? Chief Franklin's here."

It knocked the breath out of him. He felt himself going white. He glanced at Chief Miler, calmly sitting nearby.

"Can you tell me about it now?" he asked her.

"Not very well. Please hurry home. He wants to talk to you about the K-99s."

"Have the two of them met?"

"Yes, they have." She paused, as if listening to him speak, then said, "Oh, *that*! The game, honey—remember the *game*?"

"Good," he grunted. "I'll be right there." He hung up and started out.

"Troubles?" the chief called after him.

"Just a sick newt," he said, "if it's any of your business."

*

Chief Franklin's helicopter was parked in the empty lot next door when Norris drove up in front of the house. The official heard the truck and came out on the porch to watch his agent walk up the path. His lanky, emaciated body was loosely draped in gray tweeds, and his thin hawk face was a dark and solemn mask. He was a middle-aged man, his skin seamed with wrinkles, but his hair was still abnormally black. He greeted Norris with a slow, almost sarcastic nod.

"I see you don't read your mail. If you'd looked at it, you'd have known I was coming. I wrote you yesterday."

"Sorry, Chief, I didn't have a chance to stop by the message office this morning."

Franklin grunted. "Then you don't know why I'm here?"

"No, sir."

"Let's sit out on the porch," Franklin said, and perched his bony frame on the railing. "We've got to get busy on these Bermuda-K-99s, Norris. How many have you got?"

"Thirty-four, I think."

"I counted thirty-five."

"Maybe you're right. I—I'm not sure."

"Found any deviants yet?"

"Uh—I haven't run any tests yet, sir."

Franklin's voice went sharp. "Do you need a test to know when a neutroid is talking a blue streak?"

"What do you mean?"

"Just this. We've found at least a dozen of Delmont's units that have mental ages that correspond to their physical age. What's more, they're functioning females, and they have normal pituitaries. Know what that means?"

"They won't take an age-set then," Norris said. "They'll grow to adulthood."

"And have children."

Norris frowned. "How can they have children? There aren't any males."

"No? Guess what we found in one of Delmont's incubators."

"Not a—"

"Yeah. And it's probably not the first. This business about padding his quota is baloney! Hell, man, he was going to start his own black market! He finally admitted it, after twenty-hours' questioning without a letup. He was going to raise them, Norris. He was stealing them right out of the incubators before an inspector ever saw them. The K-99s—the numbered ones—are just the ones he couldn't get back. Lord knows how many males he's got hidden away someplace!"

"What're you going to do?"

"*Do!* What do you *think* we'll do? Smash the whole scheme, that's what! Find the deviants and kill them. We've got enough now for lab work."

Norris felt sick. He looked away. "I suppose you'll want me to handle the destruction, then."

Franklin gave him a suspicious glance. "Yes, but why do you ask? You *have* found one, haven't you?"

"Yes, sir," he admitted.

A moan came from the doorway. Norris looked up to see his wife's white face staring at him in horror, just before she turned and fled into the house. Franklin's bony head lifted.

"I see," he said. "We have a fixation on our deviant. Very well, Norris, I'll take care of it myself. Where is it?"

"In the house, sir. My wife's bedroom."

"Get it."

*

Norris went glumly in the house. The bedroom door was locked.

"Honey," he called softly. There was no answer. He knocked gently.

A key turned in the lock, and his wife stood facing him. Her eyes were weeping ice.

"Stay back!" she said. He could see Peony behind her, sitting in the center of the floor and looking mystified.

Then he saw his own service revolver in her trembling hand.

"Look, honey—it's *me*."

She shook her head. "No, it's not you. It's a man that wants to kill a little girl. Stay back."

"You'd shoot, wouldn't you?" he asked softly.

"Try to come in and find out," she invited.

"Let me have Peony."

She laughed, her eyes bright with hate. "I wonder where Terry went. I guess he died. Or adapted. I guess I'm a widow now. Stay back, Mister, or I'll kill you."

Norris smiled. "Okay, I'll stay back. But the gun isn't loaded."

She tried to slam the door; he caught it with his foot. She struck at him with the pistol, but he dragged it out of her hand. He pushed her aside and held her against the wall while she clawed at his arm.

"Stop it!" he said. "Nothing will happen to Peony, I promise you!" He glanced back at the child-thing, who had begun to cry.

Anne subsided a little, staring at him angrily.

"There's no other way out, honey. Just trust me. She'll be all right."

Breathing quickly, Anne stood aside and watched him. "Okay, Terry. But if you're lying—tell me, is it murder to kill a man to protect a child?"

Norris lifted Peony in his arms. Her wailing ceased, but her tail switched nervously.

WALTER M. MILLER. JR.

"In whose law book?" he asked his wife. "I was wondering the same thing." Norris started toward the door. "By the way—find my instruments while I'm outside, will you?"

"The dissecting instruments?" she gasped. "If you intend—"

"Let's call them surgical instruments, shall we? And get them sterilized."

He went on outside, carrying the child. Franklin was waiting for him in the kennel doorway.

"Was that Mrs. Norris I heard screaming?"

Norris nodded. "Let's get this over with. I don't stomach it so well." He let his eyes rest unhappily on the top of Peony's head.

Franklin grinned at her and took a bit of candy out of his pocket. She refused it and snuggled closer to Norris.

"When can I go home?" she piped. "I want Daddy."

Franklin straightened, watching her with amusement. "You're going home in a few minutes, little newt. Just a few minutes."

They went into the kennels together, and Franklin headed straight for the third room. He seemed to be enjoying the situation. Norris hating him silently, stopped at a workbench and pulled on a pair of gloves. Then he called after Franklin.

"Chief, since you're in there, check the outlet pressure while I turn on the main line, will you?"

Franklin nodded assent. He stood outside the gas-chamber, watching the dials on the door. Norris could see his back while he twisted the main-line valve.

"Pressure's up!" Franklin called.

"Okay. Leave the hatch ajar so it won't lock, and crack the intake valves. Read it again."

"Got a mask for me?"

Norris laughed. "If you're scared, there's one on the shelf. But just open the hatch, take a reading, and close it. There's no danger."

Franklin frowned at him and cracked the intakes. Norris quietly closed the main valve again.

"Drops to zero!" Franklin called.

"Leave it open, then. Smell anything?"

"No. I'm turning it off, Norris." He twisted the intakes.

Simultaneously, Norris opened the main line.

"Pressure's up again!"

Norris dropped his wrench and walked back to the chamber, leaving Peony perched on the workbench.

"Trouble with the intakes," he said gruffly. "It's happened before. Mind getting your hands dirty with me, Chief?"

Franklin frowned irritably. "Let's hurry this up, Norris. I've got five territories to visit."

"Okay, but we'd better put on our masks." He climbed a metal ladder to the top of the chamber, leaned over to inspect the intakes. On his way down, he shouldered a light-bulb over the door, shattering it. Franklin cursed and stepped back, brushing glass fragments from his head and shoulders.

"Good thing the light was off," he snapped.

Norris handed him the gas-mask and put on his own. "The main switch is off," he said. He opened the intakes again. This time the dials fell to normal open-line pressure. "Well, look—it's okay," he called through the mask. "You sure it was zero before?"

"Of course I'm sure!" came the muffled reply.

"Leave it on for a minute. We'll see. I'll go get the newt. Don't let the door close, sir. It'll start the automatics and we can't get it open for half an hour."

"I know, Norris. Hurry up."

Norris left him standing just outside the chamber, propping the door open with his foot. A faint wind was coming through the opening. It should reach an explosive mixture quickly with the hatch ajar.

He stepped into the next room, waited a moment, and jerked the switch. The roar was deafening as the exposed tungsten filament flared and detonated the escaping anesthetic vapor. Norris went to cut off the main line. Peony was crying plaintively. He moved to the door and glanced at the smouldering remains of Franklin.

*

Feeling no emotion whatever, Norris left the kennels, carrying the sobbing child under one arm. His wife stared at him without understanding.

"Here, hold Peony while I call the police," he said.

"*Police?* What's happened?"

He dialed quickly. "Chief Miler? This is Norris. Get over here quick. My gas chamber exploded—killed Chief Agent Franklin. Man, it's awful! Hurry."

He hung up and went back to the kennels. He selected a normal Bermuda-K-99 and coldly killed it with a wrench. "You'll serve for a deviant," he said, and left it lying in the middle of the floor.

Then he went back to the house, mixed a sleeping capsule in a glass of water, and forced Peony to drink it.

"So she'll be out when the cops come," he explained to Anne.

She stamped her foot. "Will you tell me what's happened?"

"You heard me on the phone. Franklin accidentally died. That's all you have to know."

He carried Peony out and locked her in a cage. She was too sleepy to protest, and she was dozing when the police came.

Chief Miler strode about the three rooms like a man looking for a burglar at midnight. He nudged the body of the neutroid with his foot. "What's this, Norris?"

"The deviant we were about to destroy. I finished her with a wrench."

"I thought you said there weren't any deviants."

"As far as the public's concerned, there aren't. I couldn't see that it was any of your business. It still isn't."

"I see. It may become my business, though. How'd the blast happen?"

Norris told him the story up to the point of the detonation. "The light over the door was loose. Kept flickering on and off. Franklin reached up to tighten it. Must have been a little gas in the socket. Soon as he touched it—wham!"

"Why was the door open with the gas on?"

"I told you—we were checking the intakes. If you close the door, it starts the automatics. Then you can't get it open till the cycle's finished."

"Where were you?"

"I'd gone to cut off the gas again."

"Okay, stay in the house until we're finished out here."

*

When Norris went back in the house, his wife's white face turned slowly toward him.

She sat stiffly by the living room window, looking sick. Her voice was quietly frightened.

"Terry, I'm sorry about everything."

"Skip it."

"What did you do?"

He grinned sourly. "I adapted to an era. Did you find the instruments?"

She nodded. "What are they for?"

"To cut off a tail and skin a tattooed foot. Go to the store and buy some brown hair-dye and a pair of boy's trousers, age two. Peony's going to get a crew-cut. From now on, she's Mike."

"We're class-C, Terry! We can't pass her off as our own."

"We're class-A, honey. I'm going to forge a heredity certificate."

Anne put her face in her hands and rocked slowly to and fro.

"Don't feel bad, baby. It was Franklin or a little girl. And from now on, it's society or the Norrises."

"What'll we do?"

"Go to Atlanta and work for Anthropos. I'll take up where Delmont left off."

"*Terry!*"

"Peony will need a husband. They may find all of Delmont's males. I'll *make* her one. Then we'll see if a pair of chimp-Ks can do better than their makers."

Wearily, he stretched out on the sofa.

"What about that priest? Suppose he tells about Peony. Suppose he guesses about Franklin and tells the police?"

"The police," he said, "would then smell a motive. They'd figure it out and I'd be finished. We'll wait and see. Let's don't talk; I'm tired. We'll just wait for Miler to come in."

She began rubbing his temples gently, and he smiled.

"So we wait," she said. "Shall I read to you, Terry?"

"That would be pleasant," he murmured, closing his eyes.

She slipped away, but returned quickly. He heard the rustle of dry pages and smelled musty leather. Then her voice came, speaking old words softly. And he thought of the small child-thing lying peacefully in her cage while angry men stalked about her. A small life with a mind; she came into the world as quietly as a thief, a burglar in the crowded house of Man.

"*I will send my fear before thee, and I will destroy the peoples before whom thou shalt come, sending hornets to drive out the Hevite and the Canaanite and the Hethite before thou enterest the land. Little by little I will drive them out before thee, till thou be increased, and dost possess the land. Then shalt thou be to me a new people, and I to thee a God....*"

And on the quiet afternoon in May, while he waited for the police to finish puzzling in the kennels, it seemed to Terrell Norris that an end to scheming and pushing and arrogance was not too far ahead. It should be a pretty good world then.

He hoped Man could fit into it somehow.